In Stillness

In Stillness

George Sifri

ARCHWAY
PUBLISHING

Archway Publishing books may be ordered through booksellers or by contacting:

Archway Publishing
1663 Liberty Drive
Bloomington, IN 47403
www.archwaypublishing.com
844-669-3957

Because of the dynamic nature of the Internet, any web addresses or links contained in this book may have changed since publication and may no longer be valid. The views expressed in this work are solely those of the author and do not necessarily reflect the views of the publisher, and the publisher hereby disclaims any responsibility for them.

Any people depicted in stock imagery provided by Getty Images are models, and such images are being used for illustrative purposes only. Certain stock imagery © Getty Images.

This is a work of fiction. All of the characters, names, incidents, organizations, and dialogue in this novel are either the products of the author's imagination or are used fictitiously.

ISBN: 978-1-4808-3893-2 (sc)
ISBN: 978-1-4808-3892-5 (hc)

Library of Congress Control Number: 2016919263

Print information available on the last page.

Archway Publishing rev. date: 02/29/2024

Also by George Sifri

A Path to Peace

An Invitation to Share:
The Companion Guide to A Path to Peace

To my children
Suzanne and David
Thank you for sharing
You have taught me so much

Stillness
A heightened state of awareness
Arising from a quiet mind
That enables one to be fully present

In stillness
We witness the miracle of life
The presence of energy
An energy of love

*There are times when I just know
I've created the moment I'm living in*

—Suzanne Sifri

* This book contains two identical versions of the same
story: one with a father and daughter and the other with
a mother and son. The mother-son version begins on page
55. Please feel free to read the version that resonates most
with you.

A fourteen-year-old girl named Rachel was walking with her father along a dirt trail in the woods. As she ventured off the path, her attention was drawn to a nearby brook where she saw something flashing in the sunlight.

She bent down along the bordering rocks and placed her hand in the cool stream. Just before grasping the shiny object, however, she noticed her reflection in the water. Something about her reflection captured her interest, and she spent some time studying it.

Several minutes later, she heard her father calling her and ran to catch up.

At dinner that night, Rachel's father, always intrigued by her spiritual curiosity, asked her what she was doing by the stream.

Rachel looked up at him and said, "I bent down to get something shiny out of the water, but as I looked closely at my reflection, I discovered something."

"What did you discover?"

"I noticed that my reflection had merged with the reflection of the surrounding trees, the reflection of the deep-blue sky, and even with the water itself. All had become one.

"At that moment, I experienced the most intense feeling of love."

"Can you tell me more about the feeling of love that you experienced?" Rachel's father asked.

"It was a love that filled me with joy … with an overwhelming sense of unity and peace. I knew that I was a part of something greater."

After reflecting on the event, Rachel continued. "It led me to understand that my energy and the energy of the universe are inseparable—that my beauty and the beauty of the universe are one and the same. I realized that there is no beginning or end, that everything is connected, that all boundaries are imaginary. The spiritual energy in one thing flows into the spiritual energy of another."

"Rachel, are you saying there is spiritual energy in everything?"

"Yes, I believe so."

After pausing to gather her thoughts, she continued. "It's not surprising if you think about it. If there is a divine presence, a divine energy, in the universe, then doesn't it seem likely that this divine energy would be present in everything?"

"I hadn't really thought about it, but yes, I suppose it does," her father replied. "And you're suggesting that we can sense this divine energy?"

"That's right. If we look deeply, we begin to see and feel the spiritual energy—to see and feel the love—within everything. Even something as inanimate as a rock has the energy of love within it.

"Of course it is easier for us to sense the love in another person, or even in an animal or plant. But when we look closely, we can see and feel love in everything.

"We can breathe in this energy.

"We can see and feel love in the wavering flame of a candle, in the ripples of a wind-swept lake, or in the rich grain of a piece of wood. We can experience love in the music of a seashell, in a cool summer's breeze, or in the sunlight as it plays upon the morning dew.

"Yet we can go even further," Rachel continued. "We can also experience love in a ceramic pitcher, a concrete sidewalk, or a bouquet of artificial flowers … all of which were created with materials from the Earth's garden.

"Love is in everything. We just need to look closely.

"For example," Rachel said, "when we look at a breath-taking sunset, we see an array of colors: deep reds, light pinks, vibrant oranges, and soft purples. We notice how these colors blend together—how one color gradually fades into another. Within this mix of light-filled beauty, we appreciate wisps of floating clouds, the sun aglow with fire.

"At first, we are captivated by the striking colors … the outline of the clouds … the peacefulness of the moment. In time, though, we come to sense something deeper. We begin to feel an intimate connection with the universe.

"In such a setting, our energy rises.

"Our feeling of love, peace, and joy rises.

"We don't need to limit ourselves to a stunning sunset, however, to feel this connection with the universe," Rachel continued. "If we look closely at something—anything—in a setting of stillness, we can see and feel spiritual energy, see and feel *love*, within it.

"For instance, have you ever looked for the beauty in a glass of iced tea?

"It is quite remarkable: to feel the cool, moist glass against your hand; to observe the melting ice transform into an array of exquisite shapes and sizes, like so many glistening crystals; to enjoy the mix of colors—the clear to cloudy ice, the light brown tea, the translucent pulp of the lemon with its somewhat darker seeds and accompanying inner white and outer yellow peel; to savor the varied flavors—the taste of the refreshing, tart lemon blended with the slightly bitter tea."

"Let me see if I have this right," Rachel's father said. "You are saying that the energy of *love* is in everything and that one way to see and feel this energy is to look closely at everything—to experience everything—in a setting of stillness."

"Yes, that's right," Rachel replied.

"But what about something as simple as the mixing spoon that comes with the glass of iced tea? Is it possible for us to sense the energy of love in that spoon?" her father asked.

"Our inclination is to label the spoon as a utensil and to think of it as nothing else," Rachel answered. "But if we take some time with the spoon, our perception changes. We feel the smoothness of its rounded surface, the roughness of its edge, the elevation of its pattern. We notice its elegant but simple design: its long stem that gradually tapers toward the cupped part of the spoon, its wide handle that provides us with a comfortable grip.

"When we rest the spoon against our cheek, we feel the coldness of its steel. When we place it in our mouth, we taste its metal.

"As we look closely at the bowl of the spoon, we see a reflection of ourselves and the surrounding light: a reflection that causes us to appear upside down if we are looking at the part of the spoon that caves inward; a reflection that provides us with a distorted image of our facial features as we peer into something that resembles a fun-house mirror."

"So you're suggesting," Rachel's father said, "that as we let go of labels and allow ourselves to fully appreciate and interact with whatever we are drawn to, we create more meaningful experiences."

"Yes," Rachel said. "What's really interesting is that we can apply this same principle to people.

"Let's take, for example, the middle-aged homeless woman standing in front of the downtown office building. As we walk by her, our attention is drawn to her greenish-brown eyes—eyes that speak of pain and despair. We notice her tattered sweater, the dirty white scarf pulled tightly around her neck, the clunky bracelet on her wrist.

"When we look directly into her eyes and offer her some money, we see her face light up with appreciation—the beginning of a smile. Her hazel eyes, now alive with hope, look deeply into our own.

"As we start to walk away, we hear the words *thank you* uttered softly. We notice a change in the air, a feeling of intimacy. We become lost in our thoughts, wondering about this woman, realizing that we have been touched by her presence."

"What do you mean, Rachel, when you say that we've been touched by her presence?"

"We've been graced by her beauty ... by the heightened energy of her appreciation."

"Are we affected by anything else during the encounter?" Rachel's father asked.

"Yes. We are also comforted by our own divine energy, by our ability to give freely and generously."

After pausing for a moment, Rachel continued. "We are reminded that such actions arise from our essence ... our essence of love."

"I understand," Rachel's father said. "When I give without reservation—when I give from the heart—it leads to the most wonderful feeling, a feeling of gentleness for all."

After reflecting on the feeling, Rachel's father asked, "What else did you come to realize at the stream?"

"I discovered in every moment that life is changing, energy is changing."

"Why is energy changing in every moment?"

"Because energy is dynamic; it is in constant motion," Rachel said. "It is continually intermingling with other energy, continually adapting, and continually evolving.

"For example, when we witness a full moon stretched wide across the evening sky or the first winter's snow, when we become still in meditation or prayer, or when we take a moment to enjoy the silence of being, our energy level often rises.

"On the other hand, when we focus our attention on things that cause us to feel fearful, such as a loved one struggling with an illness or feelings of inadequacy, our energy level often falls.

"This doesn't mean that we need to shy away from fearful thoughts and feelings," Rachel continued, "but rather that we may benefit from approaching such thoughts and feelings with increased awareness.

"For instance, when we find ourselves feeling anxious upon awakening, we can sit quietly with the emotion as we breathe slowly and deeply."

"So your suggesting that awareness plays a key role in our energy level," Rachel's father said.

"Yes, that's right," Rachel replied. "As we become increasingly aware of our feelings and thoughts, increasingly still and at peace, and increasingly trusting and mindful of the universe, our energy becomes more grounded and less susceptible to challenging events.

"For example," Rachel said, "when our airline flight is cancelled and we are able to remain centered and peaceful, we can look for the opportunity in the experience and trust that it's there. Whether it is witnessing something remarkable in the course of our delay, establishing a meaningful relationship with someone as we wait for another flight, or learning the virtue of patience, we believe that some opportunity exists. By trusting in the universe, we embrace rather than resist the change that has occurred.

"By embracing this change, we are better able to stay in the present moment—better able to notice the giggling three-year-old girl whose arms are curled around her mother's neck, better able to appreciate the elderly gentleman who is slowly but deliberately making his way to the departure gate."

"What else did you learn at the stream?" Rachel's father asked.

"I learned that if I'm not paying attention, if I'm not in the moment, I will miss the experience."

"What types of experiences would you be missing?"

After taking some time to think about it, Rachel said, "I would miss seeing the reflection of the towering evergreens and the bright blue sky become one in the stream. I would miss experiencing the beauty of unity, of energy *intermingling*, that is occurring every second ... just as the fall wind lifts the red maple leaf from its branch, twirls it playfully in the air, and lays it softly to rest on the forest floor."

"Rachel, are you saying that when I am talking with someone or simply looking at a tree that our spiritual energies are intermingling?"

"Yes. As a matter of fact, I think we can take it a step further. I would suggest that when we are thinking about others—a younger brother who is studying abroad or a recently deceased grandmother—our energies are intermingling as well.

"For example, have you ever found yourself thinking about a friend—perhaps one who lives some distance away—and then answered the phone only to find that your friend was on the line?

"Or have you ever had the uneasy feeling that a close relative—maybe someone you hadn't seen in a while—was struggling with a problem and later discovered that your relative was going through a particularly difficult time?

"Everyone and everything is connected. There are no barriers."

"How did you come to understand this?" her father asked.

"It's just something I gathered from observing the merging of my reflection with the reflection of the trees and the clouds in the stream. At that moment, I discovered that spiritual energy cannot be limited, cannot be confined. I realized that we are all a part of energy. There are no walls separating us."

"Does that mean that everyone's energy is affecting us, that everyone's energy is intermingling?"

"Yes, I believe so," Rachel answered. "When others are feeling fearful, we may feel their fear, and when we are feeling fearful, others may feel our fear. This fear may take on the form of worry, distrust, irritation, a depressed mood, anger, or even rage.

"Likewise, when we are feeling *love* and radiating it, others are often feeling it as well. As a matter of fact, when we are sending out our love with intention, with an awareness of reaching others, it can be quite powerful.

"Even more striking, however, is when we send that energy of love to ourselves, when we bask in the joy of being, and then allow that love to overflow to all in our path—like a majestic fountain emitting love-filled rays of light."

"So you're saying that our state of well-being, our feeling of peace and joy, is affecting everyone around us," Rachel's father said. "And that by feeding ourselves with love, with a sense of well-being, we are feeding others with that love as well."

"Yes," Rachel replied.

Rachel's father then asked, "Do you believe there are different levels of energy within a person? In other words, can a person be fearful on a superficial level but be peaceful on a deeper, more spiritual level?"

"Yes, I think so," Rachel said, "just as the giant oak sways with the wind yet its roots remain firmly planted."

"So, by choosing to focus on our deeper energy, can we feel more at peace? Can we take comfort in the stability of our roots?"

"I believe so," Rachel answered. "As we become still, we begin to feel the energy of *love* within. It is similar to looking at our reflection in the water. We can pass by the stream and catch a glimpse of our reflection, or we can take some time with our reflection and look deeply, feel deeply. We can make it a more meaningful spiritual experience."

"Why is stillness so important?" her father asked.

"In stillness, we feel the peace of the moment. We hear the whisperings of spirit; we become immersed in the beauty of light," she replied.

"In stillness, we are able to appreciate the spiritual energy in everything—to commune with the *love* in everything."

After pausing for a moment, Rachel continued. "More importantly, in stillness, we are able to commune with the love within ourselves. It is this love that allows us to create in the most remarkable manner, to bring forth the most wondrous experiences unto ourselves.

"We are constantly creating," Rachel added. "When we connect with love, when we choose to feel love, our energy level rises. When we connect with fear, when we choose to feed fear, our energy level often falls. This energy change affects not only us but also our world.

"When we embrace the heightened energy of love, we tend to look for the beauty and meaning in our life experiences; we connect with spirit in the gentlest of manners and radiate our love to all. In such a state, our passion and joy for life is immeasurable.

"When we allow ourselves to be encumbered by fear, we become less trusting; we tend to see ourselves as victims rather than creators of our life experiences. In such a state, we often feel overwhelmed and view life as a trial. We become distracted and miss much of what the world has to offer.

"Our energy state, however, affects more than just ourselves," Rachel continued. "When we *feel* love, we often draw out the love in others, and when we *feel* fear, we often draw out the fear in others.

"For example, have you ever noticed how uplifted you feel when someone gives you a big smile, a heartfelt compliment, or an encouraging word—how someone with high energy, loving energy, tends to bring out the best in you? On the other hand, have you noticed how being around someone who is continuously complaining, continuously criticizing, affects you—how your energy level tends to drop?

"Like attracts like. A person in a high-energy state tends to bring out the high energy in us, the love in us, while a person in a low-energy state tends to bring out the low energy in us, the fear in us.

"Our energy is affecting everyone and everything. We are not only creating—and thereby affecting—our own energy level, but we are affecting the energy level of others as well.

"What's even more amazing," Rachel continued, "is that when we quiet our minds and commune with our divine energy within, we open our hearts to the universe and invite *all of life* to interact with us. In this heightened state, we create our experiences through the joy of being; we create in a setting of pure *love*.

"This is what I experienced at the stream. As I connected with the love within and felt that love go out to everyone and everything, I entered a blissful state—a state of oneness with all.

"Many of us have experienced such blissful moments, when certain events have helped us to quiet our minds and intimately connect with love. Perhaps we were touched by the inviting smile of a child, inspired by a captivating piece of music, moved by the kindness extended to us by a stranger, or uplifted by the first blossoms of spring," Rachel said.

"But what happens if we intentionally create our life experiences by focusing our attention inward ... by communing with our *love* within?" Rachel asked.

"What happens if we become conscious nurturers of our spiritual light and come to embrace all that flows from nurturing that light?

"In such situations," Rachel stated, "we fully surrender ... fully awaken. We come to view every experience through the eyes of the soul—through loving eyes that see and feel everything, appreciate everything, with innocence and wonder."

Rachel's father then said, "So you're saying that the energy of love is within each of us ... and that by being still and consciously connecting with this higher energy, we are able to create in the most extraordinary manner, to harness this divine energy, to dance in its wonder."

"Yes," Rachel replied, "that's exactly what I'm saying."

Rachel then took her father's hands, encircled them in her own, and asked him to close his eyes. In the stillness, a mystical energy of love and light permeated her father's being.

Afterward, as Rachel's father opened his eyes, he said to his daughter, "I sensed such a beautiful energy radiating from you. I felt as if I were in the presence of the divine."

Rachel looked at her father, smiled, and said, "When we held hands, I simply acted as a mirror. I reflected your energy back onto you. It was *your* energy that you were largely sensing."

"So, what I experienced was my own energy—the spiritual light within?" Rachel's father asked.

"Yes," Rachel replied, "you were, in a way, witnessing your own reflection in the stream."

Upon hearing this, Rachel's father's eyes welled up with tears. After taking a moment to gather himself, he looked at his daughter and said, "As you told me the story of the stream, I watched you closely. I looked at your gentle brown eyes, your long dark hair, and your sweet smile. I realized that this divine being, with her gentle brown eyes, long dark hair, and sweet smile, was sharing a story with me. It was a story about *love*, a story about coming home."

As Rachel listened closely, her father continued.

"When we quiet the noise and become still, when we focus our attention on whatever we are drawn to and begin to sense the energy of love within it, we awaken. We come to see and feel the beauty in everything; we come to see and feel the beauty in ourselves. We come to embrace our love within, our beauty within, and create at the highest level … through our unity with spirit … through the joy of being.

"In such a setting, we come home to the peace of the moment … to the oneness of the universe … to the eternal from which we sprang."

I close my eyes ...
Knowing I am one with the universe ...
Realizing, in this moment, that
anything is possible

—David Sifri

A fourteen-year-old boy named Jacob was walking with his mother along a dirt trail in the woods. As he ventured off the path, his attention was drawn to a nearby brook where he saw something flashing in the sunlight.

He bent down along the bordering rocks and placed his hand in the cool stream. Just before grasping the shiny object, however, he noticed his reflection in the water. Something about his reflection captured his interest, and he spent some time studying it.

Several minutes later, he heard his mother calling him and ran to catch up.

At dinner that night, Jacob's mother, always intrigued by his spiritual curiosity, asked him what he was doing by the stream.

Jacob looked up at her and said, "I bent down to get something shiny out of the water, but as I looked closely at my reflection, I discovered something."

"What did you discover?"

"I noticed that my reflection had merged with the reflection of the surrounding trees, the reflection of the deep-blue sky, and even with the water itself. All had become one.

"At that moment, I experienced the most intense feeling of love."

"Can you tell me more about the feeling of love that you experienced?" Jacob's mother asked.

"It was a love that filled me with joy … with an overwhelming sense of unity and peace. I knew that I was a part of something greater."

After reflecting on the event, Jacob continued. "It led me to understand that my energy and the energy of the universe are inseparable—that my beauty and the beauty of the universe are one and the same. I realized that there is no beginning or end, that everything is connected, that all boundaries are imaginary. The spiritual energy in one thing flows into the spiritual energy of another."

"Jacob, are you saying there is spiritual energy in everything?"

"Yes, I believe so."

After pausing to gather his thoughts, he continued. "It's not surprising if you think about it. If there is a divine presence, a divine energy, in the universe, then doesn't it seem likely that this divine energy would be present in everything?"

"I hadn't really thought about it, but yes, I suppose it does," his mother replied. "And you're suggesting that we can sense this divine energy?"

"That's right. If we look deeply, we begin to see and feel the spiritual energy—to see and feel the love—within everything. Even something as inanimate as a rock has the energy of love within it.

"Of course it is easier for us to sense the love in another person, or even in an animal or plant. But when we look closely, we can see and feel love in everything.

"We can breathe in this energy.

"We can see and feel love in the wavering flame of a candle, in the ripples of a wind-swept lake, or in the rich grain of a piece of wood. We can experience love in the music of a seashell, in a cool summer's breeze, or in the sunlight as it plays upon the morning dew.

"Yet we can go even further," Jacob continued. "We can also experience love in a ceramic pitcher, a concrete sidewalk, or a bouquet of artificial flowers … all of which were created with materials from the Earth's garden.

"Love is in everything. We just need to look closely.

"For example," Jacob said, "when we look at a breath-taking sunset, we see an array of colors: deep reds, light pinks, vibrant oranges, and soft purples. We notice how these colors blend together—how one color gradually fades into another. Within this mix of light-filled beauty, we appreciate wisps of floating clouds, the sun aglow with fire.

"At first, we are captivated by the striking colors … the outline of the clouds … the peacefulness of the moment. In time, though, we come to sense something deeper. We begin to feel an intimate connection with the universe.

"In such a setting, our energy rises.

"Our feeling of love, peace, and joy rises.

"We don't need to limit ourselves to a stunning sunset, however, to feel this connection with the universe," Jacob continued. "If we look closely at something—anything—in a setting of stillness, we can see and feel spiritual energy, see and feel *love*, within it.

"For instance, have you ever looked for the beauty in a glass of iced tea?

"It is quite remarkable: to feel the cool, moist glass against your hand; to observe the melting ice transform into an array of exquisite shapes and sizes, like so many glistening crystals; to enjoy the mix of colors—the clear to cloudy ice, the light brown tea, the translucent pulp of the lemon with its somewhat darker seeds and accompanying inner white and outer yellow peel; to savor the varied flavors—the taste of the refreshing, tart lemon blended with the slightly bitter tea."

"Let me see if I have this right," Jacob's mother said. "You are saying that the energy of *love* is in everything and that one way to see and feel this energy is to look closely at everything—to experience everything—in a setting of stillness."

"Yes, that's right," Jacob replied.

"But what about something as simple as the mixing spoon that comes with the glass of iced tea? Is it possible for us to sense the energy of love in that spoon?" his mother asked.

"Our inclination is to label the spoon as a utensil and to think of it as nothing else," Jacob answered. "But if we take some time with the spoon, our perception changes. We feel the smoothness of its rounded surface, the roughness of its edge, the elevation of its pattern. We notice its elegant but simple design: its long stem that gradually tapers toward the cupped part of the spoon, its wide handle that provides us with a comfortable grip.

"When we rest the spoon against our cheek, we feel the coldness of its steel. When we place it in our mouth, we taste its metal.

"As we look closely at the bowl of the spoon, we see a reflection of ourselves and the surrounding light: a reflection that causes us to appear upside down if we are looking at the part of the spoon that caves inward; a reflection that provides us with a distorted image of our facial features as we peer into something that resembles a fun-house mirror."

"So you're suggesting," Jacob's mother said, "that as we let go of labels and allow ourselves to fully appreciate and interact with whatever we are drawn to, we create more meaningful experiences."

"Yes," Jacob said. "What's really interesting is that we can apply this same principle to people.

"Let's take, for example, the middle-aged homeless woman standing in front of the downtown office building. As we walk by her, our attention is drawn to her greenish-brown eyes—eyes that speak of pain and despair. We notice her tattered sweater, the dirty white scarf pulled tightly around her neck, the clunky bracelet on her wrist.

"When we look directly into her eyes and offer her some money, we see her face light up with appreciation—the beginning of a smile. Her hazel eyes, now alive with hope, look deeply into our own.

"As we start to walk away, we hear the words *thank you* uttered softly. We notice a change in the air, a feeling of intimacy. We become lost in our thoughts, wondering about this woman, realizing that we have been touched by her presence."

"What do you mean, Jacob, when you say that we've been touched by her presence?"

"We've been graced by her beauty ... by the heightened energy of her appreciation."

"Are we affected by anything else during the encounter?" Jacob's mother asked.

"Yes. We are also comforted by our own divine energy, by our ability to give freely and generously."

After pausing for a moment, Jacob continued. "We are reminded that such actions arise from our essence ... our essence of love."

"I understand," Jacob's mother said. "When I give without reservation—when I give from the heart—it leads to the most wonderful feeling, a feeling of gentleness for all."

After reflecting on the feeling, Jacob's mother asked, "What else did you come to realize at the stream?"

"I discovered in every moment that life is changing, energy is changing."

"Why is energy changing in every moment?"

"Because energy is dynamic; it is in constant motion," Jacob said. "It is continually intermingling with other energy, continually adapting, and continually evolving.

"For example, when we witness a full moon stretched wide across the evening sky or the first winter's snow, when we become still in meditation or prayer, or when we take a moment to enjoy the silence of being, our energy level often rises.

"On the other hand, when we focus our attention on things that cause us to feel fearful, such as a loved one struggling with an illness or feelings of inadequacy, our energy level often falls.

"This doesn't mean that we need to shy away from fearful thoughts and feelings," Jacob continued, "but rather that we may benefit from approaching such thoughts and feelings with increased awareness.

"For instance, when we find ourselves feeling anxious upon awakening, we can sit quietly with the emotion as we breathe slowly and deeply."

"So your suggesting that awareness plays a key role in our energy level," Jacob's mother said.

"Yes, that's right," Jacob replied. "As we become increasingly aware of our feelings and thoughts, increasingly still and at peace, and increasingly trusting and mindful of the universe, our energy becomes more grounded and less susceptible to challenging events.

"For example," Jacob said, "when our airline flight is cancelled and we are able to remain centered and peaceful, we can look for the opportunity in the experience and trust that it's there. Whether it is witnessing something remarkable in the course of our delay, establishing a meaningful relationship with someone as we wait for another flight, or learning the virtue of patience, we believe that some opportunity exists. By trusting in the universe, we embrace rather than resist the change that has occurred.

"By embracing this change, we are better able to stay in the present moment—better able to notice the giggling three-year-old girl whose arms are curled around her mother's neck, better able to appreciate the elderly gentleman who is slowly but deliberately making his way to the departure gate."

"What else did you learn at the stream?" Jacob's mother asked.

"I learned that if I'm not paying attention, if I'm not in the moment, I will miss the experience."

"What types of experiences would you be missing?"

After taking some time to think about it, Jacob said, "I would miss seeing the reflection of the towering evergreens and the bright blue sky become one in the stream. I would miss experiencing the beauty of unity, of energy *intermingling*, that is occurring every second … just as the fall wind lifts the red maple leaf from its branch, twirls it playfully in the air, and lays it softly to rest on the forest floor."

"Jacob, are you saying that when I am talking with someone or simply looking at a tree that our spiritual energies are intermingling?"

"Yes. As a matter of fact, I think we can take it a step further. I would suggest that when we are thinking about others—a younger sister who is studying abroad or a recently deceased grandfather—our energies are intermingling as well.

"For example, have you ever found yourself thinking about a friend—perhaps one who lives some distance away—and then answered the phone only to find that your friend was on the line?

"Or have you ever had the uneasy feeling that a close relative—maybe someone you hadn't seen in a while—was struggling with a problem and later discovered that your relative was going through a particularly difficult time?

"Everyone and everything is connected. There are no barriers."

"How did you come to understand this?" his mother asked.

"It's just something I gathered from observing the merging of my reflection with the reflection of the trees and the clouds in the stream. At that moment, I discovered that spiritual energy cannot be limited, cannot be confined. I realized that we are all a part of energy. There are no walls separating us."

"Does that mean that everyone's energy is affecting us, that everyone's energy is intermingling?"

"Yes, I believe so," Jacob answered. "When others are feeling fearful, we may feel their fear, and when we are feeling fearful, others may feel our fear. This fear may take on the form of worry, distrust, irritation, a depressed mood, anger, or even rage.

"Likewise, when we are feeling *love* and radiating it, others are often feeling it as well. As a matter of fact, when we are sending out our love with intention, with an awareness of reaching others, it can be quite powerful.

"Even more striking, however, is when we send that energy of love to ourselves, when we bask in the joy of being, and then allow that love to overflow to all in our path—like a majestic fountain emitting love-filled rays of light."

"So you're saying that our state of well-being, our feeling of peace and joy, is affecting everyone around us," Jacob's mother said. "And that by feeding ourselves with love, with a sense of well-being, we are feeding others with that love as well."

"Yes," Jacob replied.

Jacob's mother then asked, "Do you believe there are different levels of energy within a person? In other words, can a person be fearful on a superficial level but be peaceful on a deeper, more spiritual level?"

"Yes, I think so," Jacob said, "just as the giant oak sways with the wind yet its roots remain firmly planted."

"So, by choosing to focus on our deeper energy, can we feel more at peace? Can we take comfort in the stability of our roots?"

"I believe so," Jacob answered. "As we become still, we begin to feel the energy of *love* within. It is similar to looking at our reflection in the water. We can pass by the stream and catch a glimpse of our reflection, or we can take some time with our reflection and look deeply, feel deeply. We can make it a more meaningful spiritual experience."

"Why is stillness so important?" his mother asked.

"In stillness, we feel the peace of the moment. We hear the whisperings of spirit; we become immersed in the beauty of light," he replied.

"In stillness, we are able to appreciate the spiritual energy in everything—to commune with the *love* in everything."

After pausing for a moment, Jacob continued. "More importantly, in stillness, we are able to commune with the love within ourselves. It is this love that allows us to create in the most remarkable manner, to bring forth the most wondrous experiences unto ourselves.

"We are constantly creating," Jacob added. "When we connect with love, when we choose to feel love, our energy level rises. When we connect with fear, when we choose to feed fear, our energy level often falls. This energy change affects not only us but also our world.

"When we embrace the heightened energy of love, we tend to look for the beauty and meaning in our life experiences; we connect with spirit in the gentlest of manners and radiate our love to all. In such a state, our passion and joy for life is immeasurable.

"When we allow ourselves to be encumbered by fear, we become less trusting; we tend to see ourselves as victims rather than creators of our life experiences. In such a state, we often feel overwhelmed and view life as a trial. We become distracted and miss much of what the world has to offer.

"Our energy state, however, affects more than just ourselves," Jacob continued. "When we *feel* love, we often draw out the love in others, and when we *feel* fear, we often draw out the fear in others.

"For example, have you ever noticed how uplifted you feel when someone gives you a big smile, a heartfelt compliment, or an encouraging word—how someone with high energy, loving energy, tends to bring out the best in you? On the other hand, have you noticed how being around someone who is continuously complaining, continuously criticizing, affects you—how your energy level tends to drop?

"Like attracts like. A person in a high-energy state tends to bring out the high energy in us, the love in us, while a person in a low-energy state tends to bring out the low energy in us, the fear in us.

"Our energy is affecting everyone and everything. We are not only creating—and thereby affecting—our own energy level, but we are affecting the energy levels of others as well.

"What's even more amazing," Jacob continued, "is that when we quiet our minds and commune with our divine energy within, we open our hearts to the universe and invite *all of life* to interact with us. In this heightened state, we create our experiences through the joy of being; we create in a setting of pure *love*.

"This is what I experienced at the stream. As I connected with the love within and felt that love go out to everyone and everything, I entered a blissful state—a state of oneness with all.

"Many of us have experienced such blissful moments, when certain events have helped us to quiet our minds and intimately connect with love. Perhaps we were touched by the inviting smile of a child, inspired by a captivating piece of music, moved by the kindness extended to us by a stranger, or uplifted by the first blossoms of spring," Jacob said.

"But what happens if we intentionally create our life experiences by focusing our attention inward ... by communing with our *love* within?" Jacob asked.

"What happens if we become conscious nurturers of our spiritual light and come to embrace all that flows from nurturing that light?

"In such situations," Jacob stated, "we fully surrender ... fully awaken. We come to view every experience through the eyes of the soul—through loving eyes that see and feel everything, appreciate everything, with innocence and wonder."

Jacob's mother then said, "So you're saying that the energy of love is within each of us ... and that by being still and consciously connecting with this higher energy, we are able to create in the most extraordinary manner, to harness this divine energy, to dance in its wonder."

"Yes," Jacob replied, "that's exactly what I'm saying."

Jacob then took his mother's hands, encircled them in his own, and asked her to close her eyes. In the stillness, a mystical energy of love and light permeated his mother's being.

Afterward, as Jacob's mother opened her eyes, she said to her son, "I sensed such a beautiful energy radiating from you. I felt as if I were in the presence of the divine."

Jacob looked at his mother, smiled, and said, "When we held hands, I simply acted as a mirror. I reflected your energy back onto you. It was *your* energy that you were largely sensing."

"So what I experienced was my own energy—the spiritual light within?" Jacob's mother asked.

"Yes," Jacob replied, "you were, in a way, witnessing your own reflection in the stream."

Upon hearing this, Jacob's mother's eyes welled up with tears. After taking a moment to gather herself, she looked at her son and said, "As you told me the story of the stream, I watched you closely. I looked at your gentle brown eyes, your dark wavy hair, and your sweet smile. I realized that this divine being, with his gentle brown eyes, dark wavy hair, and sweet smile, was sharing a story with me. It was a story about *love*, a story about coming home."

As Jacob listened closely, his mother continued.

"When we quiet the noise and become still, when we focus our attention on whatever we are drawn to and begin to sense the energy of love within it, we awaken. We come to see and feel the beauty in everything; we come to see and feel the beauty in ourselves. We come to embrace our love within, our beauty within, and create at the highest level ... through our unity with spirit ... through the joy of being.

"In such a setting, we come home to the peace of the moment ... to the oneness of the universe ... to the eternal from which we sprang."

ACKNOWLEDGMENTS

I would like to thank Jim Knippling for kindly proofreading the final manuscript and for his gracious and invaluable help with the revisions that took place after publication.

I would also like to thank Larry Hughes for serving as a wonderful sounding board during this project.

I would like to extend my appreciation to Elizabeth Day and to all of the people at Archway Publishing.

I would also like to extend my appreciation to Kait Vonderhaar, Akayla Smeltzer, Kristin Gundrum, Sydney Jung, Michelle Morgan, Matthew O'Leary, and Jack Heekin for their valuable input.

I would like to thank Jenny Kane for her insightful suggestions and for her tremendous efforts in promoting the book.

I would also like to thank Raye Ann Sifri and my family (especially my mom) for their unending help and support.

Lastly, I would like to offer a special thanks to my son, David, and my daughter, Suzanne, for inspiring me to undertake this endeavor and for all of their meaningful input. Their contributions played an integral part in the writing.

ABOUT THE AUTHOR

George Sifri completed his internal medicine residency at Vanderbilt University after attending medical and law school at The Ohio State University. As a practicing physician, he developed a special interest in healing through spirituality, often conducting seminars at local universities.

He is the author of three books: *A Path to Peace, An Invitation to Share,* and *In Stillness*.

His children, Suzanne and David, continue to share their spiritual insights with him on a daily basis.

Visit him online at:
www.georgesifri.com

Printed in the United States
by Baker & Taylor Publisher Services